Hi,

Sam Kerr here, captain of t striker for Chelsea FC.

I hope you have enjoyed *The Flip Out*, *A New Knight* and *Sports Day*, the first three books in my new series, which tells how I took up playing soccer after I wasn't allowed to play AFL anymore, and how, after a rough start, I have settled into playing soccer for the Knights. And now we're playing in the finals!

The *Kicking Goals* series follows my story from a soccer newbie to a skilled striker. In these books, I share my experiences and challenges on and off the pitch, and I can't wait to share my journey with you.

I hope you love them as much as I do!

Sam

SAM KERR KICKING GOALS: FINALS FEVER
First published in Australia in 2022 by
Simon & Schuster (Australia) Pty Limited
Suite 19A, Level 1, Building C, 450 Miller Street,
Cammeray, NSW 2062

10 9 8 7 6 5 4 3 2 1

Sydney New York London Toronto New Delhi
Visit our website at www.simonandschuster.com.au

A catalogue record for this
book is available from the
National Library of Australia

ISBN: 9781761100949

Cover design: Meng Koach
Cover and internal images: Aki Fukuoka
Photo of Sam Kerr: Football Australia
Typeset by Midland Typesetters, Australia
Printed and bound in Australia by Griffin Press

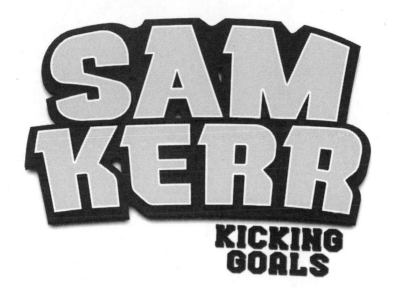

KICKING GOALS

Sam Kerr and Fiona Harris

Illustrated by Aki Fukuoka

SIMON &
SCHUSTER

London · New York · Sydney · Toronto · New Delhi

CHAPTER ONE

MY HOUSE
SATURDAY
5.30 pm

'Oh, look!' Maddi says, pointing out the window. 'They must be our new neighbours!'

As Dad turns into our driveway, we all turn to look at the family standing on the front lawn of the house next door. The Harris family moved out a few months ago and a SOLD sign went up out the front of the house a few weeks later. We've been waiting to find out who our new neighbours will be and there they are! A woman, a man and two boys – one who looks my age and the other a few years younger.

'Let's go and say hello,' Mum says, unclipping her seatbelt.

'But I need to have a shower!' I groan.

'You can say that again,' Maddi says, screwing up her nose.

We went straight from today's game against the All-Stars to our coach Ted's house for a BBQ to celebrate our epic win so, yeah, I'm not smelling my best right now.

Mum turns in her seat to look at me.

'Say hello first, Sam. Then you can have a shower.'

'Do I have to go over, too?' Levi grumbles.

'Yes, you do,' Dad says. 'It's the neighbourly thing to do.'

The four of us step out of the car and walk across the driveway that separates our two houses. Mum lifts a hand to wave as we approach them.

'Hello,' she chirps in her friendliest voice. 'You must be our new neighbours!'

The woman smiles. 'Oh yes, hello!' she says.

'I'm Roxanne,' Mum says. 'This is my husband, Roger, and our kids, Sam, Levi and Maddi.'

'Lovely to meet you all,' the woman says. 'I'm Lucy. This is my husband, Spike, and our boys, Jake and Will.'

Both boys are small and have messy brown hair that flops down over their eyes. The smallest one keeps pushing it back behind his ear, but it just falls forward onto his face again.

'They're starting at the school down the road,' Lucy continues. 'Will is in Grade Three and Jake in Grade Six.'

'That's the school where Sam goes,' Dad says, jerking his head at me. 'She's in Grade Six, too.'

'Oh, wonderful,' Lucy says. 'We've just moved from Melbourne so the boys don't know anyone here yet.'

I smile at Jake. 'I can show you around on Monday if you want?'

'Okay, thanks,' Jake says with a grin.

'I'm going there, too,' Will says loudly.

I grin. 'I can show you around too, Will.'

'Okay,' he shrugs. 'Cool.'

'Do you play soccer, Sam?' Lucy asks, nodding at my uniform.

'Yep,' I say. 'With the Knights. Our home ground is at Bruce Lee Oval, just down the road.'

'Her team won today,' Maddi says. 'It looked like it was going to be a draw but then Sam did her ambidextrous feet thing and tricked the opposition. She kicked the winning goal, which means the Knights are playing in the semi-final and if they win that game, they play in the grand final!'

I stare at Maddi, amazed. I had no idea she was paying so much attention to the game. Maddi isn't exactly what you'd call a soccer fan, so I thought she was just doing the 'good sister' thing by coming to watch me play. I'm so flattered that I decide not to tell her that in soccer it's called a 'final' not a 'grand final'. One step at a time!

I'm not the only one who's shocked. Dad arches one eyebrow at Mum and Levi makes a sound that's halfway between a snort and a laugh.

'What?' Maddi says, seeing our expressions. 'I do watch, you know! It was exciting!'

She's right. It was SO exciting. Even though the game finished hours ago my buzz still hasn't worn off. Our team played so hard to get into the finals and we did it!

Afterwards at Ted's, we couldn't stop talking about the match. We replayed our favourite moments as we sat around the table, cramming Cheezels and potato chips into our mouths.

'How about when Chelsea dodged around that All-Stars player and sliced the ball to James?' Archie said.

'Oh yeah, that was wicked!' Toby agreed.

'And that goal, James!' Ky shrieked. 'BOOM! Straight into the back corner!'

'Liam, you were on fire today!' I added.

'But your goal was the best, Sam!' Cooper said.

Okay, I'm not gonna lie … it *was* an epic goal. But it was definitely a team effort. Chelsea passed the ball to me right at the perfect moment, which is how I could make the shot. I still can't believe we're going to be playing in the finals!

'Congratulations, Sam,' Spike says now. 'That's fantastic!'

'It was a great game,' Dad says proudly, putting his arm around my shoulders. 'We're more of an AFL family, but Sam here might just turn us around.'

'Us too!' Jake cries. 'We barrack for the West Coast Eagles.'

'You're kidding!' Mum laughs. 'My other son plays for the Eagles.'

'No WAY!' Jake's eyes almost pop out of his head. 'Who?'

'Daniel Kerr,' Dad says.

Spike's face flushes red and his eyes bug out of his head. It looks like he's about to explode with excitement. 'Oh, he's sensational!'

As the adults start talking football, Levi and Maddi make a sneaky getaway back across the driveway and into our house.

Will looks up at me with eyes as big as saucers. 'Does your brother really play for West Coast?' he asks.

'Yep,' I say. 'Sure does.'

'But you don't play footy,' Will says, frowning at my uniform.

'No, but I still love AFL.'

'I don't know anything about soccer,' Jake says. 'Is it fun?'

'Heaps of fun,' I say. 'I only started playing this year, but I love it. I can teach you a bit about it if you like?'

'Cool!' Jake's expression brightens. 'Thanks!'

'Can we go inside now?' Will says, looking up at Jake. 'You promised you'd help me set up my Lego table.'

'Yeah, okay,' Jake says. 'In a minute.'

'It's okay, I have to go and get cleaned up,' I say, pulling at my dirty jersey. 'See you on Monday!'

'Come on, Jake!' Will says, tugging at Jake's sleeve.

'I'm coming,' Jake says, turning to go. 'See ya, Sam.'

CHAPTER TWO

INDI'S HOUSE
SUNDAY
4.30 pm

'Not *another* one who's sports crazy!' Indi
groans, throwing herself backwards on the
couch. 'Why couldn't your new neighbour
be into drama or reading?'

'It's all part of our evil plan to turn
you into a sports-loving nut,' I say, reaching
over from my comfy position on the
beanbag to poke her leg.

Dylan grins. 'We'll have you signing up for next season before you know it.'

'You'd have more luck turning me into a pumpkin,' Indi snorts.

It's Sunday afternoon and the three of us have spent the day hanging out at Indi's, playing board games and UNO.

'Hang on,' Dylan says. 'Aren't you the one who just exhibited your exceptional goalie skills to the whole world on Friday?'

By some miracle, Dylan and I talked Indi into being goalie for one of the soccer teams at our school's Sports Day because we didn't have enough players. She might be the least sporty person we know, but she did an awesome job and even saved a few goals.

'*Exhibited*?' I frown at Dylan. 'Isn't that what you do with art? Not sport?'

'No, it means, "to show or display",' he says.

'Alright, smarty pants!' I say, rolling my eyes. 'Just because my dad didn't give me a big fancy book full of big fancy words, you don't have to rub it in!'

'Anyway,' Indi says, sitting up. 'The only reason I "exhibited" anything was because I had no choice. You were desperate so I helped out.'

'You loved it!' I say, wriggling around on the beanbag, trying to get comfy again.

'Yeah, it was fun,' Indi shrugs. 'But I'll take green tights over those massive yellow gloves any day.'

Indi auditioned for the role of Peter Pan in our school production and got it. Dylan and I can't wait to see the show.

'Not long now!' I say, clapping my hands. 'Are you getting nervous?'

Indi bites her lip and nods. 'Yeah, a little bit.'

Dylan scoffs. 'Indi Pappas doesn't get nervous! You're gonna own that stage!'

'I don't know …' Indi shrugs.

'Hey, what's with the face?'

We look up to see Indi's older sister, Rena, standing in the doorway. You'd never guess they were sisters to look at them. Indi has curly auburn hair and glasses, while Rena's hair is jet black like their dad's. It's dead straight and hangs halfway down her back. I've known Rena since kindergarten but I always feel a bit shy around her. She's tall and pretty and wears super cool clothes. She *never* has mud on her shoes or unwashed hair like me.

'I'm starting to feel nervous about the play,' Indi says. 'I mean, what if I forget a line or fall off the stage? That would be a ... a ...'

'Travesty?' Dylan offers.

'Nice word, Dylan!' Rena exclaims.

'Thanks,' Dylan says, blushing and looking down at his shoes.

There's a loud burst of shouting from the other end of the house and we all turn our heads towards the kitchen. Indi's brothers, George, Ari and Nick, are all yelling at each other and we can hear Indi's mum shouting over the top of them to 'STOP YELLING!'

'Seriously, it's like living in a zoo!' Rena says, grabbing a magazine off the coffee table and walking out with a sigh.

Indi's house is always loud and chaotic, but that's why I love it. It's just like my own noisy house, which reminds me …

'I've gotta go,' I say, wriggling myself out of the beanbag and onto the floor. 'Mum invited Jake and his family over for a "Welcome to the Neighbourhood" dinner and I promised I'd make fudge brownies.'

'Oooh, can you save a couple for us?' Dylan says. 'Bring them to school tomorrow.'

'Sure,' I say, jumping to my feet. 'See ya.'

As I'm walking out the front door I hear George shout, 'I'm not yelling, it's ARI!'

I'm still giggling as I turn onto my street five minutes later.

CHAPTER THREE

MY KITCHEN

SUNDAY

6.30 pm

'This is delicious, Roxanne,' Jake's mum says, scooping up a forkful of biryani. 'I've only ever had a beef biryani, but the lamb is lovely.'

'Thanks, Lucy. It's my mother-in-law's recipe.' Mum nods at Dad. 'Roger's mum is an amazing cook. She does a great beef rendang, too.'

'Nana makes the best roti,' says Levi. 'World class.'

Dad's eyebrows shoot up as he turns to Levi. 'I thought you said mine was the best?'

'Did I?' Levi frowns. 'Nah, Nana's is better.'

Maddi nods. 'Definitely.'

Dad drops his fork, clutches at his heart and shakes his head in mock sadness. 'That hurts, Levi,' he says. 'That really hurts.'

As Spike and Lucy laugh, I sneak a bit of lamb to our kelpie, Penny, who's lying under the table at my feet.

Dinner with the Marriotts is going well so far. They love Mum's cooking, and we haven't had any of those weird silences we had when Dad invited his co-workers around for dinner. If we weren't sitting in total silence, they were talking about their renovations and how it was impossible to choose between the ceramic and stone kitchen tiles. I'm pretty sure Mum fell asleep at one point. Dad had to give her a poke in the side. It was the most boring night of our lives and Mum made Dad promise never to invite them over again.

But the Marriotts haven't mentioned tiles or kitchen renovations once! We've talked about school, food, movies, travel and football. LOTS of football!

'Jake and Will are looking forward to their first day at school tomorrow,' Lucy says, turning to smile at her two sons. 'Aren't you boys?'

Jake gives his mum a small nod, but he looks more nervous than excited. Will looks up at her sadly.

'Except that you can't even take us,' he frowns.

Lucy's face falls. 'I know,' she leans over and gently pushes Will's floppy fringe out of his face. 'I'm sorry, sweetheart, but we did our practice walk today and it's so close! You'll be fine.'

'Lucy and I have meetings first thing in the morning,' Spike explains.

'I can meet you out the front in the morning and walk with you if you like?' I say.

'That would be very kind of you, Sam,' Lucy says. 'Are you sure?'

'No problem!' I say.

I'm sure Dylan and Indi won't mind the boys tagging along on our walk to school. Actually, I'm looking forward to my best friends meeting my new neighbours.

'Hey, can you drive me to Stella's house after dinner?' Maddi says, turning to Levi.

Levi frowns. 'Ummm ... well ...' he stammers, trying to think up an excuse not to.

'It's Sunday night,' Mum frowns. 'Why are you studying so late?'

Maddi rolls her eyes. 'We've got an assignment due tomorrow,' she says. 'Stella's dad said he'll drive me home at ten.'

'Well, okay,' Mum says, still not looking happy about it. 'Levi will drive you then.'

'Hey,' Levi says, annoyed. 'Do I get a say?'

Dad smiles. 'No.'

'See what I put up with round here?' Levi says, nudging Jake. 'Us big brothers always get the short end of the stick with the younger ones, don't we?'

Jake laughs. 'Yep!'

Will frowns. 'What does that mean?' he says, glaring at Jake.

Lucy laughs and ruffles Will's hair. 'He's just having a joke, Will.'

I can see that Will is still annoyed but I reckon I know how to cheer him up.

'Who wants to try one of my brownies?' I say, raising one eyebrow at Will.

His face instantly brightens. 'I will!'

'*Please?*' Spike says. 'Where are your manners, Will?'

'Sorry,' Will says, blushing. 'I will, please.'

'No worries!'

I throw him a friendly grin before heading to the kitchen. It's not always easy being the baby in the family!

CHAPTER FOUR

MY STREET
MONDAY
8.40 am

'Are you sure your friends won't mind?'
Jake asks, as we set off to meet Indi and
Dylan the next morning.

'No way!' I reassure him. 'They can't
wait to meet you. I told them all about
you yesterday.'

Jake's eyebrows shoot up into his
floppy fringe. 'What did you say?'

'Relax,' I laugh. 'It was all good!'

I know how Jake feels. I get nervous when I meet new people, too, and I've only ever lived in the one house and gone to the one school. I can't imagine meeting a whole new bunch of people and starting over on the other side of the country! It must be even scarier for a younger kid like Will. I turn around to check that he's still behind us.

'Hey, Will,' I call out, 'you wanna walk up here with us?'

But he just shakes his head and keeps his eyes on the ground.

'Will's in a mood,' Jake sighs. 'I told him he could walk with us, but he said he wanted to walk on his own.'

'Oh, okay,' I say. 'I'll help you find his classroom when we get there.'

'Thanks,' Jake says with a grateful smile.

Indi and Dylan are waiting up ahead on the corner and I give them both a wave.

Indi jumps up and swishes her arm back and forth over her head like she's bringing a plane in to land. I'm suddenly worried that maybe this wasn't such a good idea after all. Indi can be pretty full-on when she's in an excited 'meeting new people' mood and it might scare Jake off. Dylan is shy, so I know he won't freak Jake out, but Indi will make up for all three of us. Maybe I should just give her a signal to tone it down a little ...

'SAM! JAKE! WILL!'

Too late.

'Hey, guys,' I call back, as Indi and Dylan walk towards us.

Dylan hangs back a little, but Indi barrels right up to Jake.

'Hi, I'm Indi,' she says with a grin. 'Sam's best friend. You're Jake, yeah?'

Jake looks a bit taken aback by the loud ball of energy that is my best friend. I have to stop myself from laughing out loud.

'Uh … yeah …' he stammers.

'And you must be Will!' Indi shouts over Jake's head. 'Hi!'

'Um, this is Dylan,' I say, finally getting a word in.

'Hey,' Dylan says quietly.

'Hey,' Jake says, smiling.

'Okay, let's go,' I say. 'We don't want them to be late on their first day.'

The others fall into step alongside me, and I turn to Indi and Dylan as we walk.

'I've told Jake about Mr Morton and ...'

'Oh, he's SO strict!' Indi groans.

'Nah, he's all right,' Dylan shrugs. 'Remember Sports Day?'

'Yeah, Sam told me how he got the PE teacher to let you play soccer,' Jake says. 'He sounds nice.'

'Just don't get on his bad side,' Indi warns, as we walk through the school gate. 'And definitely don't talk in class. He goes BALLISTIC!'

'Sam said you're playing Peter Pan in the school play,' Jake says to Indi. 'That's pretty cool.'

Indi puffs out her chest proudly. 'Yeah, it is,' she beams. 'Tickets are on sale now if you want to come and watch?'

'Sure!' Jake says.

Dylan and I grin at each other behind Indi's back. Jake has no idea what he's just done. Now that he's shown an interest in getting tickets to the show, Indi will never let him forget it.

After Jake and I deliver Will to his classroom, the two of us head to the Grade Six classroom where Indi and Dylan have made room for him at our table. The other kids keep looking over at Jake curiously, but before anyone can ask any questions, Mr Morton enters the room. He walks to his desk and throws Jake a friendly smile.

'Good morning, 6A,' he says. 'As you can see, we have a new student starting with us today. His name is Jake and I'd like you all to make him feel welcome, please.'

Everyone claps politely and Jake blushes. Chelsea and Nikita join in the applause, too. I'm still amazed at how much Chelsea has changed over the past few weeks. She still has her moments but she's way nicer than she used to be. It's taken six years, but if things keep going this way, Chelsea and I might just end up being friends. Even just saying that in my head sounds weird, but I guess weirder things have happened lately. Like me starting soccer a couple of months ago and ending up playing in the finals!

'I have an exciting announcement this morning,' Mr Morton says, clapping his hands together. 'Over the next few weeks, we are going to be learning all about objects in space. Planets, moons, the stars and constellations.'

Dylan, who has been leaning back on the legs of his chair, almost falls backwards with excitement. I reach out, grabbing his arm to pull him forward before he topples over and bangs his head on the table behind him. Indi smothers a giggle and I look away before I laugh, too. Dylan is so focused on what Mr Morton is saying, he has no idea that he almost cracked his head open.

Dylan loves anything to do with space and always has. In prep, whenever we were allowed to play with the dress-up box, he always picked out the astronaut costume. I reckon he spent half of our first year of school dressed as an astronaut. He has a huge poster of the solar system on his bedroom wall, and his mum and dad bought him a telescope for his birthday last year. In other words, a space topic is Dylan's idea of heaven!

'Your first project is going to be a 3D model,' Mr Morton continues. 'It will be exhibited as part of a science fair in two weeks' time, so this morning's task is to

find a partner and start thinking about
an idea.'

*What?! Mr Morton NEVER lets us choose our
own partners.*

Indi, of course, puts her hand straight up.

Mr Morton nods at her. 'Yes, Indi?'

'Did you say we can choose our own
partners?' she asks, speaking slowly to
make sure our teacher catches every word.

'That's correct,' Mr Morton says. A small
smile tugs at the corner of his mouth, as if
he knows this is messing with our heads.

The whole class erupts into cheers and
excited chatter.

'QUIET!' Mr Morton shouts. 'If there's
any more of that behaviour, I can easily
change my mind.'

Ah, there's the Mr Morton we know and fear!

'Now, QUIETLY begin to choose your partners and discuss your model,' Mr Morton says. 'If you need any help, you can come up to my desk and ask.'

I usually partner with Indi for everything at school, and Dylan usually goes with Harry or Cam. It's one of the downsides to being part of a group of three. But now we're a group of four, which makes it so much easier.

'How about I go with Jake and you two go together?' I suggest.

'Cool,' Indi says.

Dylan turns to Indi, eyes wide with excitement. 'I've already got a gazillion ideas!'

'Please don't tell me any of them involve building an *actual* rocket ...' Indi says.

Dylan frowns. 'Well, maybe not a life-sized replica, but ...'

Indi groans and drops her head into her hands.

CHAPTER FIVE

MY KITCHEN

MONDAY

4.15 pm

'Have you got any ideas for your project yet?' Mum asks, as she hands Jake and me our steaming hot chocolates.

'Not yet.' I turn to Jake. 'Unless you've had a massive brainwave in the past two minutes?'

Jake shakes his head. 'Nope.'

After racking our brains in class and not coming up with a single idea, Jake and I decided to keep brainstorming at my house after school. We got a *teensy* bit distracted when we first got home, after I suggested going outside for a quick kick.

'Just to wake our minds up after being at school all day,' I told Jake.

He agreed it was an excellent idea, but we ended up staying out there for a lot longer than we probably should have. Mum eventually came out to give us a not-so-subtle hint.

'Do you think you should come inside and get started on your project now?' she'd called to us from the back door.

'Yeah, okay …' I'd said, dropping the

footy on the grass and trudging inside with Jake close behind.

Now, we're both sitting at my kitchen table with a blank notepad in front of us. The only good part of being back inside is that we're super close to the yummy scones Mum just pulled out of the oven.

'Can we have some scones please, Mum?' I ask. 'They'll help our brains work better.'

'Of course they will.' Mum chuckles. 'Do you want jam with yours, Jake?'

'Oh, yes please!' Jake says. 'Thanks, Mrs Kerr.'

Mum waves an oven-mitted hand at him. 'Call me Roxanne,' she says. 'Okay, I'm going to go and do a few things in the office and leave you to it.'

'Thanks, Mum!'

'Oooohhh eeese are OOH OOD!' Jake says through a mouthful of hot, buttery scone.

'Mum makes the best scones in the world,' I say, slathering my scone with thick, creamy butter. 'Indi and Dylan always drop hints for Mum to make them when they come over.'

'No wonder!' Jake says.

'You must miss your friends back in Melbourne,' I say, suddenly realising how horrible it would be if I couldn't see Indi and Dylan every day.

Jake nods. 'Yeah, it kind of sucks but we'll be going back at Christmas, so I'll see them then.'

Christmas! I think. *That's so far away!*
I seriously would not cope with not seeing Indi
for that long.

'And I talked to my best friend on the phone last night,' Jake says. 'He's coming for a visit in the next holidays.'

'Oh, good!' I feel much happier hearing that. 'And until then, you've got the three of us to hang out with.'

Jake grins. 'Thanks, Sam. Yeah, Indi and Dylan are cool.'

'Yep, they're the best,' I say, feeling proud of my besties. 'So, what do you reckon about this project?'

'Well, I remember last year someone made a really cool 3D solar system for the science fair at my old school,' Jake says.

'Maybe we could do that? It had a sun that lit up and everything.'

Finally, an idea! YES!

'Cool,' I say, grabbing my pen and writing 'solar system' at the top of our now not-so-blank notepad. 'What do we need for that?'

'Ummm,' Jake frowns, thinking. 'We'd have to have paints, and we could use foam balls to make the planets.'

'Oh yeah,' I say, feeling my brain finally kicking into gear. 'And we could glue all the planets onto a big piece of cardboard!'

'We could have an asteroid belt, too!' Jake says.

'Yeah, and we can stick name tags next to everything!'

I'm writing everything down quickly and feeling excited about this project now. This is going to be fun!

'Hey,' Jake adds, 'what if we have information paragraphs along the bottom of the chart with definitions of "asteroid belt" and "meteors" and "comets" and –'

'Jake?'

We turn at the sound of Will's voice calling through the screen door.

'Come in!' I call.

The front door squeaks open and Will appears in the kitchen doorway a second later. He's still in his school uniform and looks so small, standing there scuffing his runners on our tiled floor, his brown hair flopping down over his face.

'Hey Will,' I say. 'Wanna scone?'

Will shakes his head.

'What's up, Will?' Jake asks.

'Can you come and help me finish the Lego rocket?' Will asks.

'Sorry, mate, I can't,' Jake says. 'I have to do homework with Sam.'

Will glares at his brother, turns and walks out.

I can't help feeling sorry for him. 'Maybe Will can help us make the planets next time we get together?' I say, once the screen door slams shut behind him.

Jake shrugs. 'Maybe,' he says. 'But he has to try and make friends his own age, too.'

'I guess,' I say.

'So, when do we wanna get all the stuff for our project?' Jake asks.

'I'll ask Mum if she can take us on the weekend,' I say. 'Maybe after my soccer game.'

'Oh, that's right!' Jake says. 'It's your finals on Saturday!'

'Yeah, I'm pretty nervous, but really excited, too.' I grin. 'It's like all the feelings at once, you know?'

'I was like that before our footy final last year,' Jake says. 'I couldn't eat for the whole day!'

'Did you win?' I ask.

'Nah, we lost by five points.' Jake looks sad at the memory. 'It was a total bummer.'

I suddenly feel even more nervous and start picking at the edges of the notepad.

'Don't worry,' Jake says. 'I bet your team is awesome. I was going to ask … would it be okay if I came to watch on Saturday? Dad loves soccer so I bet he'd want to come, too.'

'Sure! The more Knights supporters, the better.'

Jake's face lights up. 'Cool! I'll tell Dad.'

A buzz of excitement shoots through my whole body just thinking about the match. I wish it wasn't so far away! How am I going to concentrate on anything else for the rest of the wcek? It feels like waiting for Christmas morning to arrive, but even better!

CHAPTER SIX

MY FRONT YARD

TUESDAY

3.45 pm

'Hey Sam!'

I'm heading down my front path on my way to training the next afternoon when Jake calls out from next door. I look over to see him and Will building something out of Lego on their front porch.

'Hi!' I call back, slinging my soccer bag over my shoulder.

'Where are you going?' Jake says, standing up and walking over to the fence.

'Soccer training,' I say. 'I'm meeting Dylan at the end of the street.'

'Oh, right,' Jake says.

'Mum says she can take us shopping for the project stuff on Friday after school,' I say.

Jake grins. 'Cool!'

Will's head snaps up. 'But we were going to ride our bikes to the beach on Friday.'

'We can do that any day,' Jake calls over his shoulder.

'But you promised!' Will throws a piece of Lego down on the porch then stands up and storms inside the house, slamming the door behind him.

Eek! That was a bit awkward.

Jake looks embarrassed. 'So, you and Dylan walk to soccer training together?' he asks, changing the subject. 'Is it close?'

'Yeah, not far,' I say. 'I'd better go. He's probably waiting for me now. See ya!'

'Bye!'

When I turn the corner, I see Dylan hopping from foot to foot.

'Come on, Sam!' he calls. 'We don't want to be late! Ted will be *incensed*!'

'Coming!' I start to jog towards him.

Ted hates it when we're late to training. He's big on the whole 'having respect for the rest of the team' thing and reckons being late shows a lack of it for your teammates. But I've never been late one single time to training or a game in the whole time I've been with the Knights, and I don't plan on starting today!

Our coach gets us all working hard right from the start. As soon as we put our water bottles down (I've got the new one Mum bought me last week — it has little soccer balls all over it), Ted makes us do laps and gets us to pair up to practise short passes. After that, we take turns zigzagging our way through cones, keeping the ball at our toes the whole time.

Ted usually makes us do a couple of laps at most but tonight, he gets us to do the whole cones course five times. It's a cool night but, by the time I finish the last course, I'm panting like my dog, Penny, when she's been lying in the sun too long.

'Okay, everyone, grab a quick drink then we'll do some more drills,' Ted shouts, pulling hard on the brim of his lucky Victoria Park cap. 'Then we'll have a practice match!

'But before we get back into the drills, I've got a little announcement to make,' he continues, as we all flop onto the grass and suck greedily from our water bottles. 'I've been thinking about the big games we have coming up and I think it's important that one of you takes on a leadership role in the team.'

Chelsea stiffens beside me and sits up straighter. I glance over at her and know straight away that she's expecting Ted to give the role to her because she's his niece. Who knows? She could be right. But then Ted turns his face away from Chelsea and looks across to the other side of the circle.

'Dylan,' he says, 'I'd like you to take on the role of team captain for this finals season. Is that okay with you?'

Dylan is in the middle of taking a giant swig of water and I worry that he's about to spit a long stream of water out of his mouth and straight at me. His eyes widen in shock. He swallows, then lowers the water bottle and stares at Ted in amazement as red blotches spring up on his neck and face.

'Uh … yeah, sure … thanks,' he manages to stammer.

I'm so thrilled for him that I want to jump up and give him the biggest hug in the world, but I know that will only embarrass him more. Instead, I grin and give him a big thumbs up from across the circle.

Dylan might be surprised at Ted's choice but I'm not. I have a feeling the rest of the team isn't either – except for Chelsea, who looks like she's swallowed a soccer ball. Dylan's an excellent striker, but he's also smart, levelheaded and kind.

'Stay back after training and we'll have

a bit of a chat about it, okay?' Ted says to Dylan.

Dylan just nods, still looking shellshocked.

Ted claps his hands together. 'Right, everyone! I want you all to line up in front of the net for some shooting practice.'

Everyone jumps to their feet and instantly crowds around Dylan to clap him on the back and high-five him.

'Congrats, mate!' James says.

'Nice one, Mawut!' Ky grins.

'Legend!' Liam cries.

The only one who heads straight to the net is Chelsea. I guess she still has a way to go when it comes to the whole 'being nicer' thing.

I wait until everyone has moved off before giving Dylan a giant hug. 'I'm so rapt for you!' I say. 'You are gonna be an AWESOME captain!'

'Um, thanks,' he says, swiping one hand across his sweaty brow. 'Yeah, it's pretty cool.'

'What's up?' I ask. 'Aren't you happy? You're CAPTAIN!'

'I know I *should* be happy, but there's one big problem, Sam.' Dylan glances over his shoulder to make sure Ted and the rest of the team can't hear him. 'Ted just made a huge mistake!'

CHAPTER SEVEN

MY SCHOOL

WEDNESDAY

10.50 am

'Do you want the rest of my mandarin?'
I say, holding it out to Dylan. 'I'm full.'

'No thanks,' Dylan mutters, staring at
the apple in his hand and twirling the stem
back and forth between his fingers.

Indi and I glance at each other across
the table. Dylan *never* says 'no' to extra

food at recess, which means this is worse than I thought. I was hoping Dylan might feel better after a good night's sleep, but he looks more stressed out this morning than he did yesterday.

I hung back after training last night so Dylan and I could walk home together.

'Don't you want to be captain?' I'd asked him.

'Of course, I do,' Dylan said, his voice sounding tight and strained. 'I just don't know if I CAN be captain.'

'What do you mean?' I scoffed. 'Sure you can! You were captain of the Sports Day soccer team last week.'

'That was different,' Dylan said. 'That was just for fun. But this is the Knights

and we're in the finals and I can't…
well …'

'You can't what?'

He stopped then and turned to me.
'Sam, you know how shy I am! How am
I supposed to pump everyone up before a
game when I'm stuttering and blushing all
over the place?'

I scoffed and waved my hand at him.
'You'll be fine!'

But later that night, I lay in bed thinking
about what Dylan said. It is true, he is so
shy that he does blotch and stammer when
more than two people are looking at him.
The only people he's not shy around are
me and Indi, but that's only because we're
his best friends. He's going to have to

talk in front of an entire soccer team and that's going to freak him out.

'Did you tell your mum and dad that Ted made you captain?' Indi asks now, unwrapping her muesli bar.

'Yeah,' Dylan mutters, glancing up and looking across the busy schoolyard at a bunch of kids playing basketball.

'What did they say?' I ask.

Dylan shrugs. 'They were really happy and said how proud they were.'

'See!' Indi cries. 'Even *they* know it was the right choice!'

'Yeah, but now I'm even more nervous about letting them down, too,' Dylan says. That worried expression is back again.

'Hey guys!'

We look up to see Jake standing at the end of the table with a big grin on his face.

'Hi, Jake,' I say. 'I looked for you when the bell went.'

'I promised Will I'd hang out with him for the first ten minutes of recess,' Jake says, sitting down beside Dylan.

'Is he okay?' Indi asks.

Jake nods. 'Yeah, when I left him, he was playing four-square with some kids in his class. He didn't want me to go, but I told him it's good for him to make his own friends.'

I nod. 'That makes sense.'

Jake looks at Dylan then back at me and frowns. 'Hey, is everything okay?'

he asks. 'You all looked really serious when I walked up.'

'Dylan is captain of our soccer team for the finals,' I say, clapping Dylan on the back.

'That's awesome!' Jake says, turning to Dylan and beaming. 'Congrats!'

'But he's worried he won't be any good,' Indi explains. 'Dylan isn't great at speaking in front of lots of people.'

'My mouth goes dry,' Dylan says miserably, 'and I get all red and blotchy and ... well ... it's a whole thing.'

Jake nods sympathetically. 'Oh right.'

'If I just had to shout instructions to everyone on the pitch, that would be fine,' Dylan says, 'but Ted said I have to give the team a pep talk before training and games.'

That's when I have a genius idea.

'What if Indi helps you with the speeches part?' I suggest. 'She's an actor! She does that stuff all the time.'

Dylan frowns. 'I don't know …'

'Why not?' Indi asks. 'It's a great idea! I know exercises to help you relax before a performance. Same thing!'

'But I don't have your confidence,' Dylan shrugs.

'You can learn!' Indi exclaims. 'Don't be such a pessimist.'

Dylan looks surprised.

'Yeah, I know some big words, too,' Indi says smugly.

Jake and I laugh, and Dylan grins.

'Okay,' Dylan says. 'We can give it a go.'

'Cool!' Indi says. 'We'll have our first rehearsal after school.'

'*Rehearsal*?' Dylan instantly looks stressed again. 'That sounds ominous.'

'I don't know what "ominous" means, but I'm going to call it a rehearsal whether you like it or not,' Indi says firmly. 'You wanna come to our first *rehearsal*, Sam?'

'Can't,' I say. 'I told Mum I'd take Penny to the park. Do you and Will wanna come, Jake?'

'Will's got swimming,' Jake says, 'but I'll come.'

'Ace,' I say. 'You can pick up her poo for me.'

Jake looks horrified.

'She's joking!' Indi laughs.

'Am I?' I say, doing my best evil grin. 'Hey, can I have a sip?' I ask Indi, reaching across to grab her Harry Potter water bottle.

'Yeah,' Indi says. 'But didn't your mum just buy you one last week?'

'Yeah,' Dylan says, 'I remember it – it had little soccer balls all over it.'

'I know,' I groan. 'I'm too scared to tell Mum I've lost it. I thought it was in my bag, but when I checked at recess it wasn't there.'

Indi rolls her eyes. 'My mum would go crazy if I lost a new drink bottle,' she says, nudging Jake. 'How about you?'

'Uh, yeah … mine too,' Jake says, blushing and looking down at his hands. 'Umm … I should go and see Will. I said I'd play four-square with him.' He gets up and runs away from the table.

That's weird, I think. *Didn't he just say Will needs to make friends of his own?*

I catch Dylan's eye and he gives a little shrug but we don't say anything.

As soon as Jake leaves, Indi turns to Dylan. 'Okay, so the first thing we need to work on is your breathing,' she says.

Looks like the first rehearsal can't wait until after school. Indi's already started.

'It all comes from your diaphragm,' she says, leaning over to poke Dylan below his ribs. 'In there!'

'OW!' Dylan cries, rubbing the spot where Indi's bony finger pressed down. 'How is that supposed to help?'

'Well, you don't feel nervous anymore, do you?' I say, grinning. 'So, I reckon that's a pretty good start!'

Indi giggles and Dylan rolls his eyes.

'One question,' I say. 'What the heck is a diaphragm?'

CHAPTER EIGHT

THE QUOKKAS' HOME GROUND
SATURDAY
3.20 pm

It's Saturday afternoon. I'm trying to
get all my nervous energy out by tapping
the soccer ball from toe to toe in the
middle of our lounge room. It's helping
me feel better, but I don't think Maddi,
who is lying on the couch reading a
magazine, is happy about my pre-game

warm-up. She keeps glancing up at me and sighing hard enough to blow out a room full of candles.

'Just go, will you!' she finally shouts, slamming down the magazine. 'You're making me dizzy!'

'Come on,' Dad says, popping his head into the room. 'I'll drive you in early – the others can follow later.'

I've never been this nervous before a soccer game. Not even before my very first one. But this is different. This is a semi-final! All the way there, I can barely keep my legs still in the car.

'Sam! Stop jigging!' Dad says. 'It's very distracting!'

'I can't help it!' I groan.

Dad laughs. 'You'll be fine! Just think of it as a normal game, not a semi-final.'

But that's easier said than done. The word 'final' is like a huge word projected onto a super-size IMAX screen in my head. We're playing the Quokkas – one of the best teams in our division. The last time we played them we won, but not by much.

As soon as Dad pulls the handbrake up, I jump out of the car and run towards the pitch, where Ted is setting up the cones for a warm-up drill.

'G'day Sam.' Ted grins. 'Bit keen, are we? You're not due for another fifteen minutes.'

'I couldn't stay home anymore,' I say, suddenly feeling a bit silly. 'Too nervous.'

Ted laughs. 'Nerves are *good*. They give you adrenaline.'

He points at the equipment and bags lying on the concrete steps of the Quokkas clubhouse. 'Since you're here early, you can give me a hand. Could you fetch me that red bag with the balls in it, please?'

'Yep!' I sprint off, grateful to be able to do something helpful, and move my legs.

The rest of the Knights soon start arriving for warm-up and each one looks as nervous as me. But poor Dylan looks the worst of all of us. His face has a bit of a yellowy tinge, like he's about to vomit.

'You okay?' I ask him quietly.

'I'm fine,' Dylan squeaks.

'Just remember what Indi said about breathing and your diagram,' I whisper.

'*Diaphragm*,' Dylan whispers back.

'Whatever. Just remember to do it.'

As we run through our drills, I keep glancing at the Quokkas who are warming up at the other end of the pitch. They're fast and, even from this distance, I can see how fit and agile they are. This is going to be a tough game.

Our supporters start arriving and positioning themselves along the sidelines. The Knights have loads of fans here today, including our biggest little fans, the under 7s Mini-Rebels team. Their banner this week reads, *GO KNIGHTS GO!* When I give them a wave, they all squeal and jump up and down.

Indi and Jake are chatting with Maddi and Levi. My dad and Jake's dad are talking to Daniel, and Mum is chatting with Dylan's parents.

When kick-off is a few minutes away, Ted calls us over to the sidelines for his pre-game pep talk. 'The three main things I need you to focus on today,' he says, looking at each of us in turn, 'is to keep the pressure up, stay in your positions and don't crowd around the ball too much.'

We all nod and say, 'Yes, coach!'

'Over to you, Dylan.'

Dylan swallows and within moments I see red patches start to pop up all over his neck. His hands are shaking, too.

Oh no. This is not good.

'Uh … yeah …' he starts, his eyes darting all over the place. 'So … just remember to … uh ….'

Chelsea folds her arms and rolls her eyes, and the rest of the team just look uncomfortable.

'Make space and … uh … keep your for … formations and … yeah …'

His whole face has gone red now and his hands are hidden deep in his pockets.

Ted clears his throat. 'Uh, thanks mate. Okay, everyone, just remember what we talked about at training, all right? Communication, keep driving the ball forward and keep it simple. The Quokkas defence is pretty good, so find space and make yourselves available to each other. Right, get out there and have fun!'

Before Dylan runs off, Ted stops him. 'Dylan, just a sec.'

I walk slowly onto the pitch and glance back to make sure Dylan is okay. He's nodding at whatever Ted is saying, and I'm relieved to see him grin when Ted nudges him gently on the arm.

I'm heading to my usual position in right midfeld when someone shouts, 'GO SAM!'

I look over to see Jake grinning and waving at me. I give him a quick wave then turn my full attention to the ball. I'm not going to let it out of my sight for the next forty-five minutes.

The referee blows his whistle and it's on!

We won the coin toss, so the Knights take the kick-off. Cooper manages to get the ball around his Quokkas player but another, faster player quickly sweeps it out from under his feet and slices a short pass to one of his teammates in left fullback. Dylan tries to tackle the ball away from him, but this kid is good. He boots the ball towards their goal, where another Quokkas player uses his chest to cushion the ball down to his feet, before spinning and shooting for goal.

But Toby is ready for it and he easily catches it in his mitts. Our supporters go crazy, jumping up and down and screaming out, 'YES, TOBY!' and 'TAKE IT BACK, KNIGHTS!'

Adrenaline races through me and I'm dying to get in on the action. With Ted's words in my mind, I stay in my right midfield position but find empty space, ready to call for the ball at any moment. Toby throws the ball down the right-hand side of the pitch towards Chelsea, who traps it under her foot and starts to run with it. Within seconds, she's tackled by Quokkas players on both sides.

'Chelsea, I'm open!' Ky calls, sprinting down the sideline towards her.

Chelsea manages to 360-spin her way out of the tackle and boots the ball towards Ky, who taps it with his foot to trap it, then turns and runs down the sidelines with a tall Quokkas girl at his heels.

I'm in the perfect position to receive the ball so I call for it. 'KY!'

Ky kicks it to me and, with a Quokkas player bearing down on me, I get in a short pass to Dylan who, with some excellent footwork and dodging skills, gets the ball back to me as soon as I find the space. Dylan's not having any problem with his confidence now that he's out on the pitch!

I'm just ten metres out from the penalty box now, in the middle of the pitch, and in the perfect position to go for goal. The goalie is small. I know if I can get it a metre above her head, it will go straight in. A Quokkas player comes up on my right side, so I switch the ball to my left foot, drive it down a few more metres and then boot it over the goalie's head and gloves, straight at the net.

GOAL!

Our supporters go crazy, cheering, clapping and waving their banners and caps in the air. I don't believe it! I got the first goal in the semi-final.

'Backflip! Backflip! Backflip!' the mini-Rebels chant from the sidelines.

I run towards my teammates and throw myself up and over into a backflip. The mini-Rebels all cheer. I look over just in time to see Jake's jaw drop. Then my team is rushing towards me to high-five and clap me on the back.

The rest of the first half flies by and, although the Quokkas have a few shots at goal, Toby is in fine form so they don't gct a single one past him. By the time the ref blows his whistle for half-time, it's still 0–1 our way. It's a good feeling to be ahead but none of us are prepared to start celebrating just yet, especially Ted. He congratulates me on my goal then reminds us that we need to stay on top of our game in the second half because the Quokkas will be giving it their all now. At the end of his talk, I see Ted glance at Dylan, but Dylan is looking away. It's almost like he's deliberately looking anywhere but at the coach, and it's obvious to me that he doesn't want a repeat of what happened before the start of the game.

We all head back onto the pitch to start the second half, pumped to get this game going, but no one scores anything in the first fifteen minutes. There's lots of running up and down the pitch, with both teams taking possession of the ball at various points before losing it to the other team, but neither of our teams get close to the goals. Before long, all of us are exhausted.

Ted swaps out a few of us to give us a break and those of us who get our turn on the sidelines greedily slurp from our water bottles. I've only been off for a few minutes when Dylan takes his chance at a long-range goal. And it pays off! The stunned Quokkas goalie doesn't even have time to reach for the ball as it skims along the grass straight past her and into the back of the net.

The cheers are so loud that I'm sure people in the next suburb must be able to hear us. Then when the ref blows his whistle a few minutes later and we've won, 0–2, the noise from our supporters gets even louder. Ted starts doing what looks like an Irish jig right there on the sidelines. I sprint onto the pitch and launch into two more backflips, one after another, then hurl myself straight at Dylan along with the rest of my team.

Dylan is almost smothered in the avalanche of Knights bodies piling on top of him. We all end up in a huge tangle of arms and legs on the ground.

I'm lying there on the scratchy grass, trying to wriggle out from underneath Archie's sweaty armpit, and one thought keeps going round and round in my head. *I'm going to be playing in a final!*

CHAPTER NINE

MY KITCHEN
SUNDAY
5.30 pm

'Can you pass me a toothpick, please?'

'Yep,' Jake says, pulling one out of the stack next to him on the coffee table.

It's Sunday afternoon and Jake and I are working on our solar system project for the science fair. It's getting there but we've still got a lot of work to do.

We've collected all the materials, painted white orbits on a huge piece of black chart paper and stuck it onto an even bigger piece of cardboard. Today, we're making the planets and painting them is tricky. We have to stick long toothpicks into the foam ball, dip a paintbrush into the paint, then put the wet brush onto the ball and hold it still while we rotate the ball with the toothpick, so that the paint goes on evenly.

Right now, I'm making Jupiter, and Jake is cutting the rings of Saturn out of cardboard. It's fun, but unfortunately everyone in my family has an opinion on how we can make it better.

'You should use a beach ball for the sun!' Maddi said when she got home from work and saw what we were doing. 'We've got a big yellow one in the shop that would be perfect!'

Maddi works in a clothing shop at the mall. I have no clue why they would be selling beach balls but I didn't want to ask, in case she thought we might be considering her idea.

'Do you want to use fairy lights for the stars?' Mum asked when she came in to see if we wanted some snacks. 'I think we've got some in the garage.'

'No thanks, Mum,' I said. 'We're going to make them out of paper and stick them on.'

'Fairy lights is actually a cool idea,' Jake said when Mum walked out again. 'Why did you say "no"?'

'I've seen those fairy lights,' I whispered to Jake. 'They're as big as Jupiter and would look too weird.'

'Good call,' Jake nodded.

The only good idea came from Levi. He said we should make break bits off the foam and rub them on sandpaper to make jagged rock shapes for the asteroids.

'Then you just paint them brown,' he'd told us.

'It sounds like they'll end up looking like something Penny would produce in the backyard,' Maddi said, screwing her nose up.

The look on Maddi's face made Jake crack up. He might have found all the dog poo talk hilarious, but I'd had enough.

'MUM!' I'd shouted. 'Can you please tell Maddi and Levi to leave us alone?'

'Leave them in peace!' Mum called from the kitchen. 'It's their project, not yours.'

It's been nice and peaceful since then.

'There!' I say, holding up my finished Jupiter. 'How does that look?'

'Awesome,' Jake says, 'but not as awesome as your team winning the semi-final!'

'I know!'

I still can't believe it. We all went out for pizza after the game yesterday and, no matter how many times people congratulate us, it hasn't sunk in yet. Our win even made Dylan feel better about his failed pep talk. He said it just made him more determined to do a better job as captain before the final.

'I'm not going to let Ted down like that again,' he'd said. 'I'll get Indi to come over tomorrow and help me beat this nerves thing, once and for all!'

'Did you and your dad like watching the game?' I ask Jake now, twirling Jupiter around on the toothpick.

'We loved it!' Jake says. 'Dad even talked to Ted about signing me up next season.'

'That would be amazing!' I squeal.

'Well, Ted said it depends if there are any spots in the team,' Jake says, cutting out another ring for Saturn. 'But maybe

their star player could put in a good word
for me?'

'Dylan would be happy to do that,' I say.

'Not Dylan, you!' Jake laughs. 'You're
the best player on the whole team! That
first goal you shot was unbelievable!'

'Nah,' I say, embarrassed, but flattered.
'Anyway, we'll both put in a good word for
you, okay?'

'Thanks!'

I'm about to grab the next planet –
Mars – when a voice calls through my
screen door.

'Jake? Are you in there?'

'Come in, Will!' I call back.

Will appears in the doorway. He ignores
me and looks straight at Jake. 'Mum said

dinner's nearly ready,' he says. 'She said you have to come home.'

'Okay,' Jake says. 'I'll be there in ten minutes. I just have to finish this first.'

'What is it?' Will asks, taking a tiny step closer.

'We're making the solar system,' I say, holding up Jupiter for him to see. 'This is Jupiter and Jake's making Saturn.'

'Can I help you make the rings, too?' Will asks Jake.

'No, sorry,' Jake says. 'I have to do it. If you get the size wrong, it won't fit.'

Will glares at his brother before turning and running out of the house.

Jake looks at me and sighs. 'He'll be okay,' he says. 'Now, do you want me to start making the poo asteroids?'

CHAPTER TEN

MY HOUSE
TUESDAY
3.48 pm

'Mum, have you seen my boots?'

Mum walks into my bedroom to find me searching frantically under my bed, in my wardrobe and under my desk. Training starts in twelve minutes, and I can't find them anywhere.

'Your soccer boots? I thought you left

them outside,' Mum says, opening the wardrobe.

'So did I!' I say, my voice rising with panic. 'But they're not there!'

I *CAN'T* be late to training! Not today. Ted gets annoyed when we're late to normal trainings, so imagine how upset he'd be if I was late to the one before a final!

'Let me go and have another look,' Mum says, hurrying out the door.

But she can't find them either and ten minutes later, the boots are still nowhere to be found. I'm almost hyperventilating with panic. Dylan would have headed off without me by now. He knows better than to be late for Ted, especially when he's the newly appointed captain!

'Come on,' Mum says, grabbing her car keys. 'I'll drive you. You'll just have to wear your runners today.'

As we pull up to training five minutes later, the team are doing warm-up laps around the oval. Ted stands near the fence, checking his clipboard.

'You're late!' he snaps as I sprint towards him.

'I'm sorry, coach!' I pant. 'I couldn't find my soccer boots and so Mum and me were —'

'I don't want to hear excuses, Sam,' Ted glances down at my runners and frowns. 'You need to take responsibility for your belongings and make sure you have everything ready to go, well before training starts.'

'I know,' I say, looking down at the grass. 'I'm sorry.'

'Okay,' Ted says, his voice softening slightly. 'Go and join the team.'

My tummy sinks as I jog towards my teammates. If Ted thinks I'm being a slacker and not taking soccer seriously, he might bench me for the first half of the game. For a *final*!

I'm so annoyed at myself. How did I lose my boots? I've never lost shoes before! And that's on top of losing my brand-new drink bottle ... What's going on with my brain lately?

I end up jogging alongside Chelsea, who glances at me and then down at my feet.

'I've lost my boots,' I say, before she can say anything about my runners. 'That's why I'm late.'

But instead of saying something nasty, Chelsea surprises me by offering to help. 'I've got a spare pair in my bag that you can borrow. I think we're about the same size.'

I'm so shocked, I almost trip over my own feet.

On our way home, Dylan tells me about his 'rehearsals' with Indi.

'We figured out how to stop my hands shaking!' Dylan says excitedly. 'I just have to warm my body up. There's this thing Indi showed me – I flop over and touch my toes and breathe out then slowly stand up, bit by bit, until I'm straight again. Then I take a few more deep breaths and then I pat my body, legs and arms all over like I'm drumming on myself.'

'Cool,' I say, trying my best not to smile at the funny picture I have in my head of Dylan flopping about and drumming on his arms.

'I wouldn't do it in front of everyone,' Dylan says quickly, reading my mind. 'Only at home before I leave for the game. Oh, and I have to do a face warm-up, too! Like this.'

Dylan stretches his mouth and eyes open as wide as he can and does an over-exaggerated chewing motion. He looks like a camel chewing on grass.

'Um … okay …' I say carefully, still

trying not to giggle. 'So does Indi do this stuff before she goes on stage?'

'Yep!' Dylan grins. 'I know it looks weird, but it totally works. I tried it out at my haboba's house the other night. She'd made mandazis and I stood up to thank her, in front of all my family.'

'You had mandazis!' I cry. 'Why didn't you bring us any?' Dylan's grandmother makes the best mandazis in the world. They're kind of like doughnuts, and Dylan always brings one for me and Indi after a Mawut family get-together.

'There were none left.' Dylan shrugs. 'Anyway, I'm feeling really good about talking to the team before the game on Saturday now!'

Deep down, I wonder if he might feel differently when he's speaking in front of the team, but I don't want to crush his hopes, so I nod and smile. 'Great!'

'Hey, maybe you left your soccer boots in the car after the semi-final,' Dylan says, changing the subject. 'Have you looked there?'

'No, I'll check when I get home,' I say. 'But I never take my shoes off in the car, so I don't think they'll be there.' Mum always makes me leave my soccer boots outside the front door after a game because they're so dirty. I'm 99.999 per cent sure that's exactly what I did on Saturday, so why aren't they there?

'It's a bit weird,' Dylan says, as we turn into my street. 'First your drink bottle and now your boots. You don't usually lose stuff.'

'I know! I don't know what's going on lately.'

'Well … maybe,' Dylan stops, looking guilty.

'What?' I ask. 'Maybe what?'

'Maybe it's not actually you who's losing this stuff.'

I frown. 'What do you mean?'

Dylan glances over at Jake's house as we pass it and lowers his voice.

'Wasn't Jake at your house on Sunday?' he asks softly. 'And last week, when you were talking about losing your drink bottle, he got all weird and rushed off to check on Will even though he told us Will needs to stand on his own two feet.'

'You think Jake stole my stuff? But why would he do that?'

'I don't know,' Dylan shrugs. 'I could be wrong.'

'You *are* wrong!' I say, feeling annoyed as I push open my front gate. 'He wouldn't do that.'

'Okay, sorry!' Dylan says, following me up the path. 'It was just a thought.'

'Sam!' Mum calls out from the kitchen as we walk into the house. 'I found your boots!'

'Where were they?' I ask, running into the kitchen with Dylan close behind.

'In the backyard,' Mum says, nodding at the boots, which are now sitting on the ledge outside the kitchen window. 'I'm just drying them out. I found them right at the end of the backyard. They were soaking wet from the rain last night. That's why I tell you to leave them under the front porch, not out in the open.'

'But I didn't take them down there,' I say, frowning. 'I never even went into the backyard after the game on Saturday.'

I don't understand. If Mum found them at the end of the backyard, then maybe they got there another way. Maybe someone threw them over the fence?

Dylan turns to look out the window. We can hear a football being kicked against the fence of the house next door.

Jake's house.

CHAPTER ELEVEN

MY HOUSE

WEDNESDAY

5.20 pm

'Sam! Take Penny for a walk, please!'
Mum shouts when I arrive home from
Indi's house.

'Do I have to?' I call back.

Indi and I went to her house after
school so I could help her practise lines
for the play tomorrow night. It was

exhausting so all I want to do now is chill out.

'Yes, you do have to!' Mum calls back. 'It's your turn.'

Penny is already waiting at the front door. She jumped up the second she heard the word 'walk'.

I grab her lead from the hook beside the front door and Penny leaps at my heels, tail wagging and tongue flopping out of her mouth.

'Oh, hang on, Penny,' I say, remembering to grab her frisbee for the park.

I leave Penny on the front porch and run back through the house and out into the backyard. It takes a few minutes before I finally find the frisbee behind Levi's old skateboard next to the shed. I grab it and run back through the house.

'Haven't you left yet?' Mum calls as I bolt past the kitchen.

'Going now!' I call back. 'Had to get the frisbee!'

But when I yank open the screen door, Penny isn't waiting for me on the front porch.

'Penny!' I call, but she doesn't come bounding around the side of the house, and I can't see her anywhere in the front garden.

My heart leaps up into my throat. A sick feeling washes over me when she doesn't appear.

'Penny!' I shout again, frantic now. 'PENNY!'

I run around to look down the side of
the house, but there's no sign of her. Then
I see something that makes my heart start
pounding.

Our front gate is wide open.

Every worst possible thought begins
to run through my head. What if Penny
took off to the park and got lost? What
if she ran out on the road and got hit by
a car?

I run down the path and out to the
street, screaming her name as loud as
I can.

'PENNY! PENNY!'

'What is it? Where is she?' Mum comes
running up the path behind me. She looks
as panicked as I feel.

Hot tears prick at the corners of my eyes. 'She's ... I don't know ...' I manage to croak. 'I just went to get the frisbee and –'

Mum's eyes widen. 'Did you leave the gate open?'

'No! I shut it when I got home from Indi's.'

At least, I'm pretty sure I did ... didn't I? I always do. Shutting the gate is something that's been drilled into me ever since I could walk. The whole Kerr family knows to shut the gate so Penny can't get out. But there it is, wide open. So maybe I did leave it open this time?

'I'm sure I ...'

I burst into tears. If something has happened to Penny and it's my fault ...

Mum puts her arm around me. 'It's okay,' she says. 'We'll find her. Just let me turn the oven off and we'll go and look around the neighbourhood.'

'Okay,' I sob, wiping the tears off my face. 'Quick. We have to go now!'

Mum turns to run back to the house when we hear a shout.

'SAM!'

I turn to see Jake leading Penny down the street towards us, holding her firmly by the collar with one hand and wheeling his bike along with the other.

'Penny!' I cry, and run to her, burying my face in her warm, furry neck. 'Where were you?'

'I was on my way back from the park and found her sniffing at a tree around

the corner. I couldn't see you anywhere, so I thought maybe she got out.'

'She did!' Mum says, coming over to give Penny a cuddle, too. 'Naughty girl. You gave us a fright!' She turns to Jake. 'Thank you, Jake. Thank you so much for bringing her back. Penny means everything to us.'

I look up at Jake, nodding along, my head still filled with horrible thoughts of what could have happened to her.

Jake starts to blush. 'Oh, um, it's okay. I was just there,' he says, looking down at his feet.

Is the shock making me imagine things or is Jake acting a bit ... guilty?

'How about you take her to the park now?' Mum says, rubbing my arm.

'I can come too if you want?' Jake says.

I force a smile onto my face as I clip Penny's lead on. 'Sure. Let's go.'

But as we walk off down the street together and Jake starts talking about our science project, I can't stop a weird tightness from creeping across my chest.

Was Jake's timing at finding Penny just a little bit too perfect?

CHAPTER TWELVE

MY SCHOOL

THURSDAY

10.40 am

'Are you sure Jake *found* Penny?'

'What do you mean?' I ask, even though
I know exactly what Indi means because I
was wondering the same thing all last night
and this morning.

'I mean, are you sure he ... you know?'
Indi has the same expression she has when

she's worried that Mr Morton is about to tell her she got an answer wrong.

'Don't tell me you're going to start accusing Jake, too!' I say, snapping my Salada in half. 'Dylan thinks he stole my water bottle and boots, now you're saying he's into dog-napping as well?'

But that little voice in my head is getting louder. *Come on, Sam, admit it. You wondered if Jake might have had something to do with it, too.*

'It's just weird,' Dylan says. 'Jake seems cool but these things always happen when he's around.'

'You're wrong,' I say stubbornly. 'Both of you. There's no way Jake took Penny. Why would he do that? That's so mean.'

But now that the idea is in my head,

I can't get rid of it. I'm remembering how the boots were at the back of my garden, right next to Jake's fence … and how he just happened to be in the right place at the right time to find Penny …

Just thinking this way is making me feel a bit sick. 'Anyway,' I say, trying to make my voice cheery. 'There are WAY more important things to be thinking about right now, like Indi Pappas's big night tonight!'

'Woo hoo!' Dylan crows, cupping his hands around his mouth.

Indi grins and stands up to do a little half-bow. 'Thank you, thank you!' she says, pretending to be a movie star waving to her fans. 'You're all so kind for attending the world premiere!'

Dylan and I pretend to take photos of her as Indi strikes a few poses like she's on a red carpet. Finally, she collapses into giggles on the ground.

'Are you nervous?' Dylan asks with a sly grin. 'Cos if you are, I know some tricks to help you relax before the show.'

Indi swats him with her hand and rolls her eyes at me. 'Listen to Mr Confidence over here!' she says.

'I'm not,' Dylan says softly. 'I thought I was but then I was lying in bed last night, thinking about the whole team looking at me before the biggest game we've ever played and I felt like I was going to pass out.'

'At least you were already in bed,' I say with a grin.

Dylan narrows his eyes at me. 'Very funny.'

'Just do those exercises I taught you before the game and you'll be fine, I promise,' Indi says. 'I'll be doing them tonight when I'm a nervous wreck!'

'You?' Dylan scoffs. 'As if!'

'I get nervous!' Indi says. 'Especially when I'm playing the lead role!'

'I can't WAIT!' I say, clapping my hands. 'Dylan and I are getting there early so we –'

'Don't tell me anything!' Indi cries, covering her ears. 'I don't want to know! If I think about you two sitting in the audience, I'll get so nervous that no camel-chewing exercise on earth will save me!'

CHAPTER THIRTEEN

MY SCHOOL HALL
THURSDAY
7.25 pm

'I'm taking you to Neverland!' Peter Pan cries. 'You'll never have to grow up there.'

'But what would my mum say?' Wendy asks.

'What's a mum?'

'Someone who loves you and tells you stories.'

'Oh good,' says Peter Pan. 'You can be our mum!'

Everyone in the audience laughs as Indi claps and leaps around the stage.

Dylan and I got to the hall super early tonight so we could get front-row seats for the show. I'm so glad we did. I have the best view in the whole hall of Indi playing Peter Pan and she is SO GOOD!

There's one part when she's fighting Captain Hook and, for a second, I almost forget that it's Indi up there. *Come on, Peter Pan!* I think to myself. *You can beat him!*

I can't believe this talented actor on stage is my best friend. I feel so proud I could burst. I'm not the only one who's loving the show. Everyone in the audience

laughs, cheers and claps their hearts out for Peter, Wendy, the Lost Boys … and even for Captain Hook! A bunch of boys sitting behind us cheer every time Captain Hook walks onstage, while the rest of us boo and hiss.

I even forget to worry about Jake while the play is on. His family and mine walked here together tonight but when Jake tried to talk to me on the way, I found it hard to look at him. He asked a few times if I was okay, so I told him I was just nervous for Indi. What was I supposed to say? *Oh, I just can't stop thinking about the fact that maybe you've been messing with me by stealing my stuff and making me think I'd lost Penny.*

I don't think so.

When the show ends, the audience leaps to their feet to give the cast a standing ovation. When Indi comes out to take her bow, I scream louder than anyone in the whole hall. She beams at Dylan and me, and it feels like an actual celebrity is smiling at us.

'Wow, Indi was awesome!'

Dylan and I turn around to see Jake standing behind our chairs, beaming with joy.

'I had no idea she was such a good actor!' he says.

'Yeah,' Dylan says gruffly, still suss on Jake, too. 'I've gotta find my mum.'

Dylan makes his escape and Jake turns to me. 'What did you think, Sam?' he says.

'I loved it,' I mumble. 'Um, I have to go. I told Indi I'd meet her out the front.'

I know I've hurt Jake's feelings by brushing him off like that, but I can't help it. The more I think about it, the surer I am that he's been messing with me. I head towards the exit, desperate to see my best friend and give her the biggest hug in the world, when I crash straight into someone stepping out of their row.

'Watch it!' they shout.

'Oh, sorry, Chelsea,' I say. 'I just want to be the first to see Indi.'

'Yeah, well, tell her she did a good job,' Chelsea says with a shrug. 'I wasn't expecting the show to be that good.'

'Uh, yeah, I'll definitely tell her,' I say, thinking, *As IF I'm going to say that!* It doesn't matter how much Chelsea tries, she just can't help saying the wrong thing sometimes.

'Looks like your new dog-walker and his brother are trying to get your attention,' Chelsea says, nodding at Jake and Will, who are trying to make their way through the crowd of people. I can see Jake craning his neck, trying to look at me.

'My dog-walker?' I say, frowning.

'Yeah, I saw him taking your dog for a walk the other day. He was leading Penny around the block near your house.'

My tummy tightens. So it *was* Jake who took Penny! And I guess that means he probably took my boots and water bottle, too …

I'm so angry. A water bottle and boots are one thing, but Penny? How could he do that? All I can think about now is finding Jake and confronting him, right here in the school hall.

'It looked like he was struggling a bit to control her,' Chelsea says, 'until Jake came running up the street and grabbed the lead off him.'

Suddenly, it all makes sense.

CHAPTER FOURTEEN

MY SCHOOL HALL
THURSDAY
9.30 pm

I know what I need to do but first, I need
to find my best friend.

There's a crowd of people standing
around Indi as I walk out into the foyer.
She breaks away from them and runs over
the second she spots me.

'Was I okay?' she cries, grabbing

my arms. 'Did you like it? Could you tell when I nearly tripped over after the Lost Boys scene?'

'You were AMAZING!' I throw my arms around her and squeeze her hard. 'I was SO proud of you! You are the BEST Peter Pan in the WHOLE WORLD!'

Indi squeals and jumps up and down. 'I saw you and Dylan as soon as I came out! I can't believe you were in the front row!'

'I'm sorry,' I say, laughing, 'but we didn't want to miss a thing!'

Dylan runs over to give Indi a hug. 'You were so good!' he says.

'Good?' Indi laughs. 'With that big vocabulary of yours, you're gonna give me "good"?'

'Okay, you were super-excellent, super-eminent, exceptional and superb.' Dylan grins. 'How's that?'

'Perfecto!'

Jake and Will are standing on the other side of the foyer with their parents and mine. Jake glances over at the three of us and he looks so sad that I decide I can't wait a second longer. I need to sort this out, once and for all.

I turn to tell Indi that I'll be back in a minute, but she's been surrounded by her whole family, who are making enough noise to bring the whole roof crashing down on top of us.

I can hear her dad shouting, *'MY LIGO SOÚPER STAR!'* at the top of his lungs as I make my way across the crowded room.

'There you are!' Mum says as I walk over to join them all. 'Did you find Indi?'

'Yep,' I nod. 'She's over there in the middle of a Pappas scrum.'

Mum and Dad both laugh. 'We'll go over and give her our congrats,' Mum says. 'She really was very good.'

'We'll come, too,' Jake's parents say.

The four adults walk over to Indi, but as Jake and Will go to follow, I stick my arm out to stop them.

'Hey, can I talk to you two for a sec?' I ask.

Jake goes pale and Will looks like he's about to cry.

'It's okay,' I say quickly. 'Maybe we can go outside?'

Will looks at Jake, who nods, and the two of them follow me outside into the cool night air. I lead us away from the school hall and over to one of the benches in the yard.

I sit down and take a deep breath. 'I just wanted to ask you about —'

'I took your drink bottle,' Will splutters. 'And I took your boots and I took Penny, but I wasn't going to hurt her, I was just going to take her for a walk and … and … I wasn't going to do anything to Penny!' Will is really crying now. 'I just wanted to give you a scare. I love dogs!'

Poor Will looks so small and sad, sniffing into his sleeve.

Jake puts his arm around his brother.
'I thought you'd probably figured out that
it was Will from Chelsea,' Jake says.

'Yeah, she told me she saw Will with
Penny,' I say gently.

'Will was upset at me,' Jake explains.
'And he took it out on you. But he knows
he did the wrong thing.'

'I was just, just … angry cos you took
Jake away and –' Will sobs.

'I told you,' Jake says in a firm voice. 'Sam
didn't take me away. I can be friends with
someone and still hang out with you, too.'

'I know,' Will sniffs, wiping his nose on
his sleeve.

'Did you know Will was doing this stuff,
Jake?' I ask.

Jake looks embarrassed. 'Yeah,' he says. 'I caught him throwing your boots over the fence and then I saw him taking Penny down the street, so I chased him to bring her back. I told Will he had to tell you after your final,' Jake says, going redder by the second. 'I didn't want to stress you out before that.'

'I was going to tell you, I promise,' Will says, looking down at his scuffed runners.

'I believe you, Will,' I say. 'It's okay. Sometimes, being the youngest can suck, can't it?'

Will stares up at me, eyes wide under his floppy fringe, and gives me the tiniest nod.

'I'm the youngest, too, so I know what it fcels like,' I say softly. Will gives me the tiniest of smiles.

'Come on,' I say. 'Let's go back inside.'

CHAPTER FIFTEEN

MY SCHOOL HALL
FRIDAY
2.00 pm

The whole class is buzzing with excitement. Our boring school hall has been transformed into an 'Objects in Space' extravaganza and it looks amazing!

Jake and I are in the corner of the hall, standing next to the display of our 3D solar system. Dylan and Indi are set up next to us with their awesome satellite model. Mr Morton was especially impressed with the number of solar cells they stuck on it.

'Wonderful detail,' he told a beaming Dylan and Indi when they brought it in this morning. 'It must have taken a long time to stick all of those on!'

'Yeah, like my WHOLE Sunday!' Indi had whispered to me.

I giggled, knowing that Mr Perfectionist would have made sure every single one of those cells was arranged in perfectly straight lines.

Our project isn't as perfect as theirs, but still, Jake and I are pretty chuffed with our solar system. It has not one, but two suns! For the first one, we used one of

Dylan's old, punctured soccer balls and painted it red with yellow splodges all over it. But the second sun is the coolest. We stuck a light bulb inside a big, round glass jar. We haven't turned it on yet – we'll do that once we've got a small crowd around us. There are lots of other solar system projects, but I reckon ours is the best.

'Okay, Grade Sixes!' Mr Morton booms. 'I'm going to let the students in now. Have fun!'

Mr Morton opens the doors to the hall and students from all the different years flood inside. A few kids gather around our table and Jake starts to explain the asteroid belt. I spot Will hovering at the back of the group and I have an idea.

'Hey, Will!' I call over the other kids' heads. 'Can you come here and help us with something?'

Will looks surprised but starts making his way towards us.

Jake leans over to me. 'What's going on?' he whispers.

'You'll see,' I whisper back.

'We need someone to do a very important job for us,' I say, as Will joins us behind the table. 'Everyone, keep your eye on the sun!'

I lean down and whisper to Will, 'Can you flick that switch over there for us?'

Will nods and reaches over to press the button. As he does, the sun lights up, casting a lovely golden glow over our project.

'Cool!' one kid at the front says.

'Awesome!' says another.

'Pretty!' squeal a gaggle of prep kids.

Jake gives me a gentle nudge. 'Thanks,' he says, then raises his voice for everyone to hear. 'Thanks, Will! Good job!'

A few kids clap before wandering away to look at the next project. Will beams with pride.

'Nice one, little bro,' Jake says to Will.

'Your project is really good,' Will says shyly.

'Thanks,' I say. 'Hey, wanna have a kick with me and Jake after school?'

'Um, maybe,' Will says. 'But I might be going to Teddy's house, so I'll tell you later.'

He wanders away to look at the other projects. Jake and I turn to look at each other in amazement.

'I think we just got dumped!' I say, raising my eyebrows at Jake.

'Yep!' Jake laughs. 'How good's that!'

CHAPTER SIXTEEN

MY HOUSE

SATURDAY

6.00 am

I wake up bright and early ... TOO bright and early. When my eyes fly open at six o'clock, my first thought is, *IT'S FINALS DAY!*

I leap out of bed and, even though the game is hours away, I immediately grab my soccer uniform. As I yank up my soccer shorts, I think for the millionth time this week how unbelievable it is that I only started playing this sport a few months ago. It feels like I've been playing soccer my whole life.

Quietly, I creep out of my room and down the hallway towards the back door while the rest of my family are still sleeping. I have this sudden need for fresh air and to move my body.

Maybe I should do some star jumps to get all this nervous energy out of my system? Or maybe I could …

'HI, SAM!'

I jump at the sound of the loud, high-pitched voice breaking the early-morning silence. Looking up, I see Will smiling down at me over the high wooden fence that separates our houses.

'Oh, hi Will,' I say, walking over and grinning up at him. 'What are you doing up so early?'

Will shrugs. 'I'm always up early,' he says. 'Jake, too.'

Jake's head pops up next to Will's. 'Hi!'

I laugh at the sight of their two floppy-fringed heads above the fence. 'What are you two up to?'

'Not much,' Jake says. 'You nervous about the game today?'

'Yeah,' I say. 'Super nervous.'

'Don't be!' Jake says. 'I've seen you play and you're awesome!'

'Yeah,' Will says. 'Jake told me how good you are. He says I should come watch you today, too. I can't wait!'

'Hey,' Jake says. 'Why don't you come over here and we'll have a kick with you? I know we're not proper soccer players or anything, but we could be your practice buddies. Our backyard isn't as big as a soccer pitch, but it's pretty huge.'

'Really?' I ask. 'That would be great!'

'We can practise with you all day if you like!' Will says.

'Thanks,' I say, laughing, 'but I should probably save some of my energy for the actual game!'

'Come on,' Jake says. 'We'll open the side gate for you.'

Both heads disappear, and I hear them noisily running down the side of their house. Smiling, I grab my soccer ball from the back porch and head off to meet my new friends for a kick.

CHAPTER SEVENTEEN

THE KNIGHTS' HOME GROUND
SATURDAY
1.25 pm

'Today is about staying focused and working as a team,' Ted says, as we huddle around him on the sidelines. 'You all know what to do out there.'

It's ten minutes until kick-off and my whole body is tingling with nerves and excitement. We're playing the Avengers today and they're a strong team. Last time we played them we lost but, when Ky brought it up during our warm-up, Ted quickly shut down any negative talk.

'Today is a different day. We're going to go out on that pitch and give it our best shot,' he said in a firm voice.

It feels like everyone in East Fremantle has come to watch our two teams play today.

All the families of the Knights players are standing and sitting in chairs along the sidelines, including mine, and I can also see Indi, Jake, Will and Spike. I'm so grateful to Jake and Will for practising with me all morning. It was exactly what I needed to take my mind off my nerves and they both learnt a lot about soccer. If he's still keen, Jake will be more prepared to join the Knights than I was.

Ted finishes his pre-game pep talk, then turns to nod at Dylan. 'Dylan, over to you.'

Come on, Dylan, I think to myself. *You've got this!*

But I can already see those red blotches popping up on his neck, and his hands starting to twitch nervously. Oh no! Not on final day! I have to do something.

'Um, Ted, before Dylan talks, can I ask a favour?' I say, desperately hoping this is going to work.

My teammates all turn towards me with curious expressions on their faces.

'Sure, Sam,' Ted says. 'What is it?'

'Well ... uh ... it's just that I've been doing this thing before games at home, and I forgot to do it this morning,' I say, feeling my own face flushing red with everyone staring at me. 'It helps with my nerves, and I thought maybe we could all do it together since it's a special game.'

'What is it?' James asks.

The side of Dylan's mouth is starting to twitch. He knows exactly what I'm about to do.

'It's a bit weird,' I say, 'but I pat my body all over ...' I bend over and start drumming all the way up my legs, over my tummy, up each of my arms and then down my whole body again. 'Up and down like this, and it helps relax me and get me focused at the same time.'

To my surprise, everyone starts copying me. Even Chelsea.

'Hey, this is cool!' Cooper grins.

'Yeah,' Liam says. 'I totally get why you do this!'

'Ace!' I say, even though the only one I care about is Dylan. He's going through the actions way more vigorously than anyone else, and I almost jump with delight when his red blotches begin to disappear.

'Good one, Sam,' Ted says. 'Thanks for that tip. It's always good for us to learn new ways to help with nerves before a game.'

'Yeah, thanks, Sam,' Dylan says in a strong, firm tone he's never used around our team before. 'So, look, I just wanted to say good luck for today and remind all of us to pick up our players and pass the ball up the pitch as much as we can. Keep it simple. The Avengers will be all over us so, when we have possession, we'll need to hold onto the ball. Let's keep talking to each other out there and don't be afraid to take shots when you can, especially if you're central and outside the penalty box.'

Everyone stares at Dylan in amazement. None of the Knights have ever heard Dylan say more than three words in a row off the pitch and now here he is, giving us all an awesome pep talk. Indi and I have always known how good Dylan is with words, big

and small, but not many other people do. Even Ted looks shocked.

'So let's do this,' Dylan finishes. 'Go Knights!'

'*GO KNIGHTS!*' we all cheer.

I clap Dylan on the back as we run out onto the pitch alongside each other. 'That was a pretty good speech back there,' I say.

'Thanks,' Dylan grins. 'And thanks for ... y'know ...'

'Huh?' I grin. 'Don't know what you're talking about. Have a great game, captain!'

'You too!'

Moments later, the ref blows his whistle, our supporters cheer and the game is on!

The Avengers come out kicking. They take possession of the ball straight away and their passing accuracy is amazing. Our defence is good, so Ky, Liam and Chelsea are all keeping up with their opposition players, but within seconds the Avengers have the ball down at their end. Luckily, Toby is on high alert and is watching the ball like a hawk so, when one of their players shoots for goal, he smacks it away and we all breathe a huge sigh of relief.

I can tell already that this is going to be a tough game, but that only motivates me more to get the ball down our end and keep it there until we score a goal.

'HEADS UP, KNIGHTS!' Ted yells from the sidelines.

'PUSH IT UP THE PITCH!' Dylan calls out.

Archie gets the ball and carves open their defence, kicking the ball to Chelsea. Chelsea takes the ball and runs with it down the left side of the pitch.

'TAKE IT ALL THE WAY DOWN, CHELSEA!' Ted shouts.

With an Avengers player hot on her heels, Chelsea turns and slices the ball to Liam, who is right outside the penalty box. He traps the ball under his foot, then pulls back and kicks it straight into the left side of the net.

GOAL!

Our supporters send up a huge cheer and Ted leaps up and down, hugging Jack and Ky beside him on the sidelines. We all sprint over to clap a stunned-looking

Liam on the back. I guess I'd look like that, too, if I scored the first goal in a final!

But Liam's goal has given the Avengers a huge jolt of determination and motivation, and over the next ten minutes they score two goals back-to-back. The ball just seems to fly down the pitch, back and forth between their players. It all happens so fast that, before we know what's going on, the score is 1–3 their way and the ref is blowing his whistle for half-time.

It's a total downer to have got the first goal and now be two goals down. I can feel our confidence as a team shrinking by the second as we all trudge off the pitch towards Ted.

'It's okay,' Ted says, as we gather around him while one of the dads hands out orange wedges. 'They blindsided us in that first half, but we can still win this.'

'We've gotta talk to each other and keep the pressure up,' Dylan says, grabbing an orange wedge and taking a big suck. 'Their defence isn't as strong as their passing, so we have to keep possession of the ball as much as possible. Like Ted said before the game, keep it simple, yeah?'

The second half starts, and from the get-go I am right in there in the middle of the action. It's our kick-off and within seconds I take possession of the ball and run straight down the centre of the pitch towards our goals. I'm instantly surrounded

by Avengers players, and there's no way
I'm going to make it all the way, so I slice
a long but fast pass to Chelsea, who is open
and running down the pitch on my right.
She sprints down the side for a few metres,
the ball at her toes, before passing it to
James, which is when I finally find open
space and call for the ball.

'JAMES!'

He swivels around and gets the ball
back over to me but, just as I trap it
under my left foot, a tall Avengers player
appears from nowhere and knocks it out
from under me, taking off down the
pitch. Dylan is right there beside her.
He manages to get the ball back before
pivoting with it and heading back towards

our goals. I'm there for him and Dylan and I do some quick-fire passing down the pitch until we see an opportunity to get it to Chelsea, right beside the goals. I have to dodge and weave around three Avengers players until I have a clear line of sight to Chelsea.

'SAM!' she screams, running out into an open space right in front of goals.

I pull my foot back and boot the ball straight to her. She doesn't even trap it under her boot, just turns and kicks the still-moving ball straight into the far corner of the net.

GOAL!

Chelsea and I turn to each other, yelling with surprise and delight, and suddenly we're running towards one other with our hands up for a high-five.

'YES!' I shout as our hands slap together.

'WOO HOO!' Chelsea screams.

I keep running past her and launch straight into a backflip, right in front of the goals. The Avengers goalie looks so shocked that, for a second, she seems to forget we've just scored a goal against them and gives me a little clap.

The game starts again and this time the Avengers take possession right off the bat. They pass it back and forth easily and quickly down the pitch. Just when we are all bracing ourselves for them to score again, Noah swoops in and stops the ball from going in the net.

Phew! That was close.

He boots the ball long and high over the heads of the Avengers, getting it as far away from their goals as he can.

A waiting Toby heads the ball straight to me. I slice a pass to Dylan, who runs straight towards goals.

'GO DYLAN!' Indi shouts.

And he does! Before the Avengers goalie knows what's happened, the ball is sailing past her gloves and into the net.

GOAL!

Everyone claps and cheers and bangs Dylan on the back, but he grins and waves us all away. 'Come on, there's not much time left,' he tells us as we crowd around him. 'Let's get one more goal and win this game!'

We run back to our positions. A few seconds later I find myself sprinting alongside an Avengers player, trying to get possession of the ball, when I see an opportunity. My foot shoots out and I manage to flick the ball away from him, then pivot on my heels to head back the other way.

'GO SAM!' Jack shouts as I toe the ball down the field.

'KEEP MOVING FORWARD!' Ted screams.

I run for a bit before passing to Ky. He dodges around three Avengers players then gets the ball to Liam, who is running open along the right side of the pitch. I run as fast as I can down the pitch and position myself directly in front of the goal. Liam kicks a high ball to me, and that's when an Avengers player runs out in front of me, putting his hands up at the wrong moment, and the ball hits his hands.

'FOUL!' The cry goes up from at least half the Knights supporters. The referee agrees. It's a penalty shot to us.

'Take it, Sam!' Dylan calls.

I look around and see that everyone on the team is nodding in agreement. Suddenly, I feel a bit sick.

I've never taken a penalty shot before, and what a way to begin. If I miss this, we could lose our chance to win the final. It's way too much pressure. But it seems like I don't have a choice.

'TAKE IT, SAM!' Ted yells.

I look over to see my family, Indi, Jake, Will and the rest of our supporters all clapping and nodding at me with smiles on their faces.

'YOU CAN DO THIS, KERR!' Indi screams.

'GO SAM!' Will cries.

'GO SAMMY!' Maddi screams.

'COME ON, SAM!' Dad yells.

The referee throws me the ball. I place it on the ground. The world seems to go completely silent as I stare down at the ball, then back up to a spot at the back on the net.

There, I think. *Right there. That's where you're gonna go, ball, you hear me?*

The goalie looks like she has other ideas about where that ball is going to go. She crouches down, hands out, ready to grab it.

It's now or never!

I take a deep breath, jog backwards, take one more look up at the net, then run forward and boot the ball straight into the corner of the net.

'YES!' Dylan screams, running towards me.

'NOTHING WRONG WITH THAT!' Ted yells.

It feels like I've just scored a goal in the World Cup. The whole team is going wild, and it feels like I'm in a dream as they all crowd around to slap me on the back and hug me.

Then the whistle blows to end the game. I instantly snap out of that dream state.

WE JUST WON THE FINAL!

'YEEEEEES!' I scream at the top of my lungs, jumping up and down and hugging my teammates. I'm so full of joy and adrenalin and excitement that I just take off, running in circles around the end of the pitch, flipping over into backflip after backflip. I circle back around to join the rest of the team who are all now on the sidelines with our coach, families and friends, hugging each other and screaming.

I feel myself being lifted up. The next thing I know I'm being hoisted up onto Dylan's and Ky's shoulders.

'Three cheers for Sam!' Dylan cries.

'Hip hip hooray! Hip hip hooray! Hip hip hooray!' everyone chants.

I jump off their shoulders and down onto the grass, shouting, 'Three cheers for Dylan!'

'Hip hip hooray! Hip hip hooray! Hip hip hooray!' everyone shouts again.

'AND THREE CHEERS FOR THE KNIGHTS!' Ted yells, throwing his red cap in the air.

'Hip hip hooray! Hip hip hooray! HIP HIP HOORAY!'

The whole team plus all our supporters and families join in on that last one and it's the loudest chant of the whole day.

Before I know it, Indi is launching herself at me. The two of us fall in a screaming, laughing heap on the grass.

I can just make out Jake and Will beaming down at me through the haze of Indi's mop of hair. They are both giving me the thumbs up. I manage to wriggle my hand out from under Indi's arm to give them a thumbs up back.

'You did it!' Indi screams into my face. 'You won the final! How does it feel?'

Well, that's easy. It's the best feeling in the whole world.

ABOUT SAM KERR

Sam Kerr is the captain of the Australian women's national soccer team – the Matildas – and a leading goal scorer for Chelsea in the English FA Women's Super League. She burst onto the W-League scene as a fifteen-year-old playing with Perth Glory. In 2016, she played for the Matildas at the Olympics in Brazil, and she was the top goal scorer in the 2017 Tournament of Nations. Since joining Chelsea in 2019, Sam has positioned herself as one of the best female strikers in the world. She was named 2018 Young Australian of the Year. In 2021, Sam became the Matildas' all-time top goal scorer at the Tokyo Olympics, and she is currently preparing for the FIFA Women's World Cup to be held in Australia and New Zealand in 2023.

ABOUT FIONA HARRIS

Fiona Harris is an Australian actor and author who has written numerous children's book series including the *Super Moopers*, *Trolls* and *Miraculous*. This is her fourth book in the Sam Kerr *Kicking Goals* series. Fiona has also written a picture book with AFL star Marcus Bontompelli and is the author of two adult fiction books, *The Drop-off* and *The Pick-up*, both adapted from her internationally award-winning comedy web series, *The Drop Off*. Fiona has co-written and starred in TV sketch comedy shows including *SkitHouse* (Channel 10), *Flipside* (ABC TV) and *Comedy Inc — The Late Shift* (Channel 9) and was head scriptwriter on ABC3 TV's *Prank Patrol*. For more information on Fiona Harris please visit fionaharris.com.

COMING SOON!

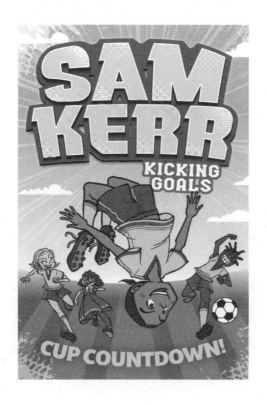

Available in print, eBook and eAudio
in April 2023.

Read on for a sneak peek!

CHAPTER ONE

KENNEDY BAPTIST COLLEGE
MONDAY
12:40 pm

'I'm starving!'

'Me too,' Indi says. 'Wanna get a sausage roll? My shout.'

'Yep!' My mouth starts watering just thinking about all of that yummy crusty goodness. 'I'll buy next week.'

Indi nods. 'Deal!'

We finish packing up our desks and are just heading out of the classroom when Dylan appears in front of us, stuffing a handful of potato chips in his mouth.

'Are ooo guys 'etting uh bus home?' he mumbles through the sound of crunching.

'Gross!' I say. 'Wanna put a few more chips in your mouth before you speak next time?'

Dylan nods and shove another handful in his gob. 'Oooo rr oou?'

His eyes almost bulge out of his head, as he struggles to keep all the chips in his mouth.

'Yes, I'm getting the bus,' I laugh.

'Not me,' Indi says. 'I've got rehearsals.'

Dylan winces as he gulps the mountain

of chips down his throat. 'Okay, see you at the bus stop after school, Sam.' He glances at his watch. 'Astronomy Club commences in two minutes!'

Dylan signed up for the Astronomy Club on the day we started high school last year. Indi and I have no clue about anything to do with astronomy, so we're happy our friend has found a bunch of people who are as mad about it as Dylan is. They love using big words like Dylan, too.

It's been cool watching our mate get more confident over the past year. He was so shy in primary school that he could barely say two words to people he didn't know. But since we started at Kennedy Baptist College, he's totally come out of his shell.

'Come on, Sam,' Indi says, as Dylan runs off. 'Let's get those sausage rolls before the canteen runs out!'

We dump our stuff in our lockers, and as we start sprinting across the yard, I think about all the cool stuff that goes along with being at high school, like yummy canteen sausage rolls, getting the bus with Indi and Dylan every day and having our own lockers. But there's not so cool stuff too, like doing more tests and having heaps more homework.

I still can't believe that Indi, Dylan and I are in Year Eight already. It's kind of weird being the young ones at school again. There are some things I miss about my old primary school, like being the oldest in the school and not having to do tests and stuff. Believe it or not, I even miss Mr Morton sometimes! Luckily, there are awesome teachers at Kennedy, too.

Dylan is in a different class to me and Indi, but the three of us are still best friends and hang out every recess and lunchtime. Unless Dylan has Astronomy Club or Indi has rehearsals. Indi's love for acting hasn't changed and she even got a small role in this year's Kennedy Baptist school play. She was a bit upset when she didn't get a bigger part but felt better when another kid told her that the older students always get the main roles. It's the same with some of the sporting teams. I really wanted to join the co-ed soccer squad but

I have to wait until next year when I'm in Year Nine. It's annoying but at least Dylan and I still get to play with our team the Knights.

We're in the U13's now, but even more exciting than that is that I'm team captain! Ted stayed our coach when we moved up to U12's and then U13's and at our first training session this year, he made the big announcement. Everyone was super happy for me, even Chelsea, and I was stoked!

Me, Sam Kerr, captain of the Knights! I still can't believe it.

Best of all, the World Cup starts in just four weeks! Dylan and I are PUMPED to see the Socceroos play! We're going to take turns watching the matches at each other's houses. The games are played in Germany, but we can still watch them on TV. Indi said she'll come over and watch the games with us. She doesn't care about soccer like we do, but she never misses the chance for a pizza night with her besties.

I've even drawn a huge chart, with all the matches, times and dates in the World Cup, and stuck it on my bedroom wall. Like, for example, I know from my chart that Australia plays Japan on Monday 12 June at 3 pm (9 pm here). When my sister, Maddi, saw my chart she sighed and shook her head.

'Obsessed much?' she groaned.

Okay, so maybe I am a teensy bit obsessed, but so what? Anyway, I know

Maddi was just taking her Year Eleven stress out on me and my World Cup chart. My sister has a TONNE of homework and most nights she doesn't even come out of her room until after I'm already asleep. I'm dreading getting to Year Eleven and having that much homework. Year Eight homework is bad enough, not to mention that massive maths test I have next week.

Bleugh!

At least I have the World Cup to look forward to!